And so the Story Goes

Jennifer Fisch-Ferguson

Fisch-Ferguson

Cover Design Credits: Tri-Crescent Photography

Editor: J. Arthur's Publishing– JAEdits.com

Copyright © 2016 Jennifer Fisch-Ferguson

ISBN: 978-1945642012

Fisch-Ferguson

Table of Contents

Long Ago

A great while ago, when the world was full of wonders and stories were spoken aloud, a strange occurrence began. As the artists, buskers and bards filled the world with their creativity their energy met with the Universe's approval. Over time the energy grew and a dimension was created to hold all of the stories ever told, currently told and those yet to come. Each version created a new energy pulse and over time these spun out into new realms. Each story changed just enough to give characters new life and some weren't happy with their past or fated destinies.

The stories are still told, but as the world turned, they became fixed as creativity moved from spoken art to written text. People began to forget that the stories had hundreds of tellings and other cultural significance. Every time a story was read, it seemed to become more and more charming, for it is with stories as it is with many people: they become better as they grow older. But not all were fond of the change; their discontent grew and provided enough energy to make a change. But they forgot what was lost and before the world became as it is today the realms lost touch with each other. And so the story goes...

Two young women walked into a large Victorian style house and looked around at the opulence. A large ornate run lay on gleaming hardwood floors. The hallway got its light from a crystal chandelier and had sconces to match on the walls. As they craned their necks, they saw a banister curling up to a second floor. Paintings lined the walls and the only sounds heard were the soft strains of classical music.

"Are you sure we are in the right place?" Kari asked. "I don't hear anyone else. Isn't this supposed to be some kind of rush party? What does the invitation say again?"

Redmondi looked at the satiny piece of paper in her hands. She then looked around and shrugged.

"Yes. This is the address. We can't be the only two invited to this rush. Keep walking, we'll find the others. And if not, this just might be the sorority for me."

The two young women walked in past the foyer and saw lights flickering from a room down a darkened room. They followed it to a room, where a tea service sat on a table. Two other young women were already seated and turned to look as they entered.

"Kelli? Mimi? What are you doing here," Redmondi asked, stunned.

"Hey, I thought you two said rushing a sorority was stupid," Kari said at the same time.

The suitemates stared at each other for a few moments. The petite blonde put her tea cup down and smiled.

"What I said is 'Who rushes in their senior year?' It's a stupid idea for people getting ready to leave," Kelli shrugged her shoulders.

"And we didn't rush, we were invited," Mimi agreed with a grin. "You might as well sit, the invitation said 9 p.m. There's tea and cookies."

The women sat back in silence. Despite having lived with each other for the past two months, they were still strangers. They had met because of a mistake, which managed to happen on Move-In day—also known as—the most hellish day before senior year starts. As if the experience of moving onto campus weren't bad enough, this particular time became downright hellish. Mistake upon mistake had been made and soon the quartet found themselves sitting in the office of the Director of Housing. The pudgy man coughed and cleared his throat.

"Okay, Ladies," he started. "The only option left is a suite open in Pruitt Hall."

He preemptively flinched after his announcement, but was met with blank stares.

"Because of the magnitude of mistakes made in your housing assignments, you will only be billed half."

Four sets of unblinking eyes narrowed in irritation almost simultaneously and he continued on.

"What appears to have happened is your applications got lost," he rushed on as the hostility became palpable. "The good news is the suite is ready for you to occupy immediately. Again I apologize for the mistakes."

"But I'm a senior. I'm supposed to have an efficiency."

"I'm a senior, I was guaranteed a single."

"I'm an upperclassman, I applied for a studio."

"Don't seniors get preference?"

All four young women hurled questions at him simultaneously, overlapping each other as the frustration was given voice. He waited for them to quiet before addressing them again.

"Normally, yes, upperclassmen get preferential housing bids. However, it's not always perfect. But the good news, is we found a suite for you all," he gulped and spoke faster because of the glares trying to set him on fire. "We can add on a free meal plan for the year. There's nothing else we can do."

After sighing was done, he pushed the contracts out on his desk and waited for the signatures. He gritted his teeth as a few of the women pressed harder than necessary and gouged his Cherrywood desk.

He led them across campus and to the top floor of a dormitory built in the 1960's. He opened the door and handed keys to each woman. He forced a smile on his face.

"Thank you ladies, have a good final year."

The words were said as he didn't bother to hide his hurried steps away from them. They watched him retreat before opening the door to their new abode, after fighting with the key, of course.

The women walked into the room and loud sighs of disgust followed. A small living room, which had a tiny loveseat as the only means of seating, lay directly ahead of them. To their right were the bedrooms and a bathroom.

They went to the living area and looked at each other. It took only a few seconds before the silence became unbearable. A tall, lithe woman with short, dark, hair in a chin length bob and dark brown eyes spoke up first.

"Well since Mr. Small and Grumpy didn't bother to introduce us, I'll go first. I'm Kari. I think we can survive the year if no one exhales too deeply. I wanted a studio apartment. Somehow this is smaller than it would have been."

A giggle burst out of the woman with long curly blonde hair, reaching almost to her waist. She stood almost five foot tall, looked all of sixteen and the lavender eyes peering out from under lush lashes missed nothing.

"I'm Kelli. Like half this University, I'm a business major. Two more semesters and I'm done. At least we'll be cozy in the winter. I can't believe this mess."

The next woman nodded and gave a warm smile. Her mocha skin complimented her hazel eyes and full lips. She cleared her throat before speaking with a husky voice.

"I'm Redmondi. Like the rest of you, I'm a senior, just waiting to graduate and be done. I'm also a night person."

"Great," Kari exclaimed. "We can room together. Unless either of you…?"

"I'm Mimi, and you are welcome to the night owl. I'm very much a morning person—which of course happens after coffee. I think this will be fine."

The last young woman's exotic looks were stunning. She had rich auburn hair, cobalt eyes, and sculpted cheekbones. They all looked around, as Mimi sighed.

"Well, I'm fairly certain it can't get worse," Mimi said with a shrug. "Lunch anyone? I made a pan of macaroni and cheese."

The rest of the group nodded. It took only two minutes for the antique microwave to spark and plunge the apartment into darkness. One by one, they broke into laughter

"I think we tripped the fuses," Redmondi said.

"This sucks, but we can make it work," Kelli said once she caught her breath. "How about we go out for pizza? My treat."

After laughing about the memories created by the odd housing situation, the women sat chatting for the remaining time. None of them had ever rushed a sorority before, so they had no idea what to expect, but speculated plenty. The invitations had showed up two weeks prior, and instructed them to the house.

"I kinda expected there to be more than four of us," Kari said. "Seems like the other houses, we passed along the way, had at least thirty giggling girls."

"Well, I like the exclusivity," said Kelli. "We are seniors and only have one year left. They must really want elite people. I have no problem being part of a select group."

The sun hung low in the sky and faded with the last of the warmth the fall would offer. The quartet sat waiting; looking around at every sound. A clock began to chime and after nine chimes, nothing happened. They looked around again, and in the doorway a tall woman stood, seemingly just appeared.

She had pure silver hair cascading over her shoulders from long twisted strands on top of her head. Not the tarnished gray of the elderly, but shiny silver that caught the last of the sunlight and reflected it. Her hair fell past her waist in gentle waves and swayed as she moved closer. Her eyebrows were light brown, but only served to set off delicate rounded features. Eyelashes batted gentle as she winked at the women from almost colorless irises. The presence of her willowy form could have been intimidating, however it was comforting. All four sat in quiet anticipation, waiting for her to speak.

"Thank you all for coming. I'm sure you have many questions, but I hope to be able to answer them all. First of all, yes only four of you were invited. We're not really a sorority at least not like the other ones around here. Think of this as more of a select association. You're all exclusive because of who you are," the woman held up her hand to stay the interruptions starting to creep in and continued. "Your participation is by choice, and you won't be coerced into staying. But before the night's end you'll have to decide whether or not you wish to stay with the group."

The women exchanged looks between them, and then back to the woman in charge. Kari sat back and took another sip of tea.

"Okay, I haven't scared you away yet. I'm going right to the point; all I ask is for you to wait until I'm done before you ask all of your questions."

The four young women nodded.

"Once upon a time, no don't roll your eyes at me. Once upon a time stories were the most revered way of passing information. Fairy Tales, as you know them, have always been important. Just think of how long they've been around; in every culture. They provide a transcending insight that had lasts through the ages and have hundreds of versions telling the same universal story."

The woman paused as she walked over to the tea service and poured herself a cup.

"Why are stories so important, you wonder? Fairy tales admit what people try to avoid and confirms what children have known all along. Life is hard, adults don't get it and there's always something waiting to hurt you."

"Well this is uplifting," Mimi muttered.

"I offered you the truth…and a tea party, but never once did I offer to blow rainbow sprinkles up your ass."

Kari and Kelli nearly choked in their cups. Mimi laughed softly and Redmondi just shook her head.

"The good news is fairy tales offer more than most adults remember. Not only do they offer cautions and a sense of morals, but more importantly it reminds kids to embrace their sense of valor and exploration. And if you are brave enough to see the trial through, you will always stand the victor. This gives little voiceless bodies a much needed way to understand the world around them, as well as their own potential."

"I'm sorry, but fairy tales are gruesome horror fests that scare kids into behaving," Kari snorted. "I don't recall any of them giving kids a way to prepare for a world filled with crime and ugliness."

The other women nodded in support.

"It's because so many parents don't want to inflict pain on their children. But because they try to sugar coat and sanitize everything, they send them into a world where conflict, drama and problems are overwhelming. The good news is that children are smart and they understand the idea of perfection is fake, and eventually seek out the truth, and find their way to fairy tales."

"And?" Kelli prompted. "I'm sure you didn't invite us here to tell us about the history of fairy tales."

"Not at all. Stories, oral history, if you will, hold the energy of creation. Stories are used to communicate what's important to a culture in any given time. The problem is that once we moved from telling stories, to writing stories, creation splintered. Each version of the story kept its individual energy in its own space."

Silence filled the room, except the gentle slurping as the woman took a long drink from her tea cup. Looks were flung between the women, and eventually their heads bent close to each other. Harsh whispers filled the room and then dropped suddenly. Four pair of eyes pinned the woman to where she stood.

"Why tell us this?" Redmondi asked.

"We're in just another realm of stories. However, someone has learned how to cross through the worlds. They are causing energy ripples and chaos. The Council has decided that we need to have some agents to help figure it out," she said.

"So you want us to work for you?" Mimi asked.

"Yes, but there's more. You need to be woken."

The ladies looked at each other. The word was simple, but carried a pulse of power they could feel.

"In full disclosure, I've never tried this before," the woman said. "No one has. But we need to do something before the realms are fractured."

"Who are the 'we' you keep referring to? Who are you?" Mimi asked.

The others nodded skeptically with her.

"The Council is a group of Fairy Tale elders that have remained aware of the other realms. How and why are the reasons we don't know. But they are always around to make sure things are running how they should," she said and then chuckled. "I'm surprised none of you have figured out who I am. I'm your Fairy God-Mother."

Redmondi groaned and Kari uttered an impressive array of curses in various languages.

"Prove it," Kelli said.

"As long as you don't expect me to sing while I do it," FGM said. "Let's see. Huh, too bad there aren't any mice around."

"I almost laughed," Mimi said, the cookie she held fell and shattered on the floor.

"Such cynics," FGM said.

She produced a thin stick from apparently nowhere. The wand moved in circles, as FGM fixated on the powdery crumbs that slipped between the crevices of the wood floor. The crumbs rose in a swirling mist and landed back on Mimi's plate.

FGM flicked her wrist and a shower of sparks fell from the ceiling. They landed on the tea service and became more cookies.

"So much better than a pumpkin carriage," Kelli said.

"Okay, then, what do we have to do?" Kari challenged more than asked.

"There is a ritual that opens each of you to your true essence. If you agree to do this mission, you will have the knowledge of who you are."

"And what do we get out of it?" Redmondi asked.

"Well, for starters, you get to leave the peanut shell of a space you live in and move in here. All bills past and present will be taken care of. Plus you get a bonus at the end when it's all done. You have a few moments to make up your minds. This can't be undone, so you need to be sure."

FGM walked out of the room, leaving them to talk. The women spoke in hushed whispers go back and forth with the pros and cons. Ten minutes later a decision had been made. The women stood, with the intention of finding their odd host. A bright flash of light made them take a step back, and a large circle of stones had replaced where the sofas sat before.

"Are you a witch?" Mimi asked nervously.

"Fairy," FGM said with a smile. "Even though you still have a lot of unanswered questions, you're doing the right thing."

"If you're not a witch, why are you doing a spell?" Mimi asked.

"In every fairy tale there is a spell of some kind," FGM said. "I promise there are no nefarious intentions here. You, four, are the heroines."

She waved the women into the circle and made them stand back to back. She placed around each of their necks and handed them a small vial to drink.

"The spell only works if you are willing. Ready?"

They nodded.

"Drink the vial and relax. As the warmth fills you, I want you to focus on this: Stories are teachings handed down from the beginning of time and will never cease, because what they mean, is different for every person, because every person receives the information in their own way."

The quartet tipped their heads back at the same time. And waited. Kelli looked around and then stared at FGM.

"Now what?"

The combined voices of four young women wailing in pain soon filled the room. All of a sudden it stopped and the only sound came from soft gasping breaths.

"What the hell was that?" Kari growled.

"All of your stories combining into your consciousness as memories. Because we don't know who or what version of them you'll have to fight, you need the advantage of unfettered information."
"Unfettered information," Redmondi mocked under her breath. "Speak to us in plain English. What's going on?"

"You all have the lead in a fairy tale story. You're all some of the strongest, smartest women out there. More importantly your characters haven't been morphed into some vapid, helpless victims."

"Who are we, really? All I'm getting are pictures of oatmeal."

FGM grinned and as she laughed looked like a delighted child as she clapped her hands.

"Kelli, you were once known as Goldilocks. It explains your affinity for safe cracking. It also explains your forever blonde hair, despite your attempts to color it. "

Three heads faced Kelli, who merely shrugged her shoulders and flipped a golden curl over her shoulder.

"A girl has to have a job. But is there any reason why I need to look like a sixteen year old?"

"Well you've always been written as a little girl. I'm sure you'll appreciate it when you're fifty."

FGM moved on to the next girl.

"Mimi, long ago was Gretel. And yes, your brother Harvey is Hansel."

"Well, that clarifies a lot," Mimi said with a shake of her head. "Am I ever going to free of babysitting him? And is this the reason I tend to dress like a Ren Faire Gypsy?"

"Well the babysitting is kind of written in, but the clothing choices are all yours. The good news is that at least one of your tales made you a complete badass fighter."

FGM turned and encountered a skeptical head tilted look.

"Redmondi, yes, you're Red Riding Hood."

"But I'm black," Redmondi protested.

"Yes, you are," FGM said.

"But the fairy tales show her as a white girl."

"Because they were written by white men."

"This leads us to Kari, better known as Puss in Boots."

The Latina's woman face went from white to red to a violent shade of mauve, and her voice came out a strangled snarl.

"I'm a cat?"

"Of course not, actually in the Straparola's original tale, you were a fairy in disguise as a cat to help the youngest son. Others of course adopted and adapted the tale."

"What stick was up Perrault's ass?" Kari asked.

"You, kind of, ermmm, left him to travel the world."

"Jilted love. Well that's a good reason," Kari nodded, and the smiled at her friends. "I'm apparently so damn good, he adapted a whole story about me."

Red scoffed, while Mimi and Kelli laughed.

"I would suggest you all move into the house immediately," FGM said. "There are wards and protections around it. Over the next few days your memories are going to come in. We're not sure what the side effects might be. In addition, since you're now on this path, new opportunities will start to come your way. You're going to need to check in with each other. Even though we know something bad is coming, we don't know where or when."

"Woah, wait a minute. We might not be safe?" Kelli asked.

"Have you ever read a fairy tale where some kind of monster or villain wasn't present?" FGM snorted in laughter. "My suggestion would be for you to read all the versions you can find about yourselves. The knowledge, skills and talent are in your head, but it doesn't hurt to get a head start."

The young women looked around at each other and then began laughing.

"So we went from being seniors in a pitiful living situation to misrepresented fairy tale heroines that need to save this world before a big baddie fractured reality," Red choked out. "Please tell me there's a beer or wine somewhere in the mythology."

FGM laughed long with them.

"There are some perks of being a fairy," she pulled a ruby colored flask from a pocket in her dress.

"No way!" Kelli said. "I want to be able to make flasks appear."

"Hell, I'd just settle for a dress with pockets," Mimi said.

"You can get a flask from any random dollar store. Bring it to me after and I'll make sure the adult beverage of your choice never runs out. Now go back to that tiny hovel they call a suite. Two Princes and a Van will be there tomorrow morning to move you," FGM grinned. "Yes, there are some really nice perks. Here is my emergency contact. I need to let the elders know you all are on board. Welcome my lovelies; this is going to be interesting."

She turned in a slow circle and with a shower of sparks disappeared.

The women looked at each other and began to laugh.

Curiosity killed the cat

Kari looked at the newly emailed offer of a job and sighed. In some ways it made her feel good that her clients would refer her to others. She had worked hard to make sure people would trust her skills as a private detective. On the other hand, she did get tired of chasing cheating partners. The novelty of catching people in the act had lost its shock factor. At this point she knew the majority of her cases would either be insurance fraud or scummy people, but it never amazed her how terrible people could be.

"Are you coming?"

She looked up as Kelli stuck her head in the room. She raised an eyebrow at her roommate, asking for more information.

"Seriously? Our weekly check in? Come on Kari, at some point you're going to have to see how amusing it can all be."

"Okay, Goldilocks, explain the ha-ha funny to me. FGM drops this bomb in our laps, and the rest of you crazy-chicks are all good with it. You were portrayed as an opportunistic thief, Mimi as an abandoned orphan and Red as naïve jail bait," she grated out. "But me? The one person in the tales shown to be smart and cunning? I'm turned into a freaking cat? These Grimm boys better be happy they are damn dead or disembodied or something. What a pair of misogynistic limp dicks. They were so intimidated by the notion of a strong female they destroyed it with their stories. And made me cat. The tongue in cheek slight of my name wasn't missed either."

Kelli walked into the room and shut the door softly. Kari met her eyes and waited.

"I know we were jerks," she said. "I think we were all in shock at FGM's announcement. But heck, you actually have the best story. Cat or not. You don't have to babysit, you aren't being stalked and you don't flirt with being arrested. Out of all of us, you're the one who took the initiative and did something."

Kari stood up and walked up to her friend.

"Promise me when we're done with this that we're going to hire a real writer to tell our stories. A female at that."

She didn't want to continue to be upset with her friends, especially since there wasn't a point to it. They had laughed at her and had put card food in front of her at breakfast. Otherwise, everyone had been too freaked out to do much more. None of the stories were good ones.

"Done," Kelli said. "I'm also thinking, if we ever get a do-over in another story and realm, I'm not rushing the damn sorority."

"Somehow, I think this new chapter already has been written somewhere. Always and already, right?"

The women high-fived and went to meet their housemates for the weekly meeting. Ever since the fog had lifted and FGM had explained everything to them, the quartet had been waiting for something weird to happen. Kari almost wished it would. She had wisely stacked her courses to be harder in her first two years so her senior year would be a cake walk, she only had a capstone course each of her last two semesters, and the rest of her courses were filler.

"Let me respond to this client and I'll be right down."

Kelli left and Kari prepared to accept the job. Her phone buzzed as she sent the email and when she looked, she found another new job offer. She had been getting more and more job offers since the awakening and it had been nice. She sent a reply and walked out for the meeting.

"Okay, let the meeting come to order."

Three sets of eyes met Red's and after a pause, they burst out laughing.

"Seriously?" Kari grinned. "You're going to try to be all serious? You're not even our leader. And in at least one version you got eaten."

"Are your tight boots making your cranky?" Red laughed back. "Fine, let's just do this. Anyone have anything to report?"

The women burst into laughter again. Kari made a silly face as Red tried to look irritated.

"Sheesh, Red. Lighten up a bit," Kelli said. "Nothing is new and interesting. Heck, even mid-terms don't even feel intimidating."

Kari sat back and looked at her suitemates. Even though, they now understood how everything had been orchestrated. She was still amazed at her life. Two months ago, she had wanted an efficiency apartment, so she could crash in between work and school. Now she not only shared a gorgeous and huge house, but also had three amazing roommates. It was the best change her life had had.

"Well now that business is done, what's for lunch?" Mimi asked.

"Sorry chickens, I just got a job nibble. It's another emergency, so I'm going to meet her right away and charge her double," Kari grinned.

"You are still on for dime drinks tonight?" Kelli asked.

"Are you still a clepto? Of course I am."

She walked back into her room, before something could be thrown at her. Lock picks were pretty darn sharp and she always had some around. Her computer chimed as she sat down. She smiled as she opened the newest offer. It, of course, was frantic.

She called the number and smiled as it rang.

"May I please speak with Dawn?"

"Is this Kari?"

"Yes, I just got your email," Kari affirmed.

"Well, I emailed ages ago. I even had time to take a nap before you called. No matter," the airy voice said in a fluid rush of words. "Anyhow, can you take the case? I absolutely need to know what's happening to my merchandise."

She made the mental note to charge Dawn at least triple price. A serious upgrade for the insult and because she could already tell the woman would be continual high maintenance. It was one the benefits of not posting a price list on her website.

"I'm free to meet with you today. Will two o'clock at Café Aroma work for you?"

"Darling girl, what part of emergency did you not understand? I'm only twenty minutes away. See you soon. Ta."

Kari blinked more than once at the fact that the woman had hung up on her. Shaking her head, she grabbed her backpack and headed out. The café was only a ten minute walk, ensuring she would beat Ms. Crazy there. She arrived with enough time to set up and grab some water.

She knew the moment Dawn walked into the room. The flighty frenetic energy preceded her. Kari had deliberately sat in the back corner so she could watch people coming and going. As she watched the tall willowy blonder weave through the crowds of tables, she realized Dawn had picked her out as well.

It surprised her, since she had learned to dress to blend in. As a private detective her best skill was being not noticed. Her short black hair was covered with a plan brown wig. The shoulder length weave was pulled back into a low ponytail that didn't enhance her face at all. With some creative make-up artistry she was able to downplay her natural beauty.

The first time Kelli had seen her get ready for work, her mouth had hung open.

"You're the only person I know who uses make-up to look less than."

"Thank you," she said, meaning it.

While Kelli, as Goldilocks, had been portrayed as kid with wild blonde corkscrew hair, the adult version was a far different story. Her long blonde hair and cute elfin like face had made men trip over themselves on a daily basis. If Kari had been attracted to women, her roommate certainly would have caught her eye. So she took the compliment as it had been intended.

"Kari, darling," Dawn said, throwing air kisses in her general direction. "You really should think about using a tanning bed."

The smile plastered on her face, kept the string of insults from coming out of her mouth. Kari had spent her entire life being not Latina enough in her community. Thanks to some dalliance a few great grandpa's back in her lineage, she had gotten light brown eyes, almost blonde hair, which she kept dyed ebony, and a complexion that let her pass. However, she'd never been called pale. Her apparent distaste for the meeting must have given her a pallid complexion.

"Dawn, so good to meet you."

Kari chanted about the customer always being right as a mantra in her head, even as she quadrupled her price.

"Of course it is my dear. I have a job you must take immediately. I am hiring you to track a shipment of heirlooms that has been stolen from Morning's Light Fuseau Co. That's my antique business. *Garcon.* I need a coffee here."

Dawn's entire monologue was said as she shook Kari's hand and sat down. To her amazement, the barista did come from behind the counter and take the coffee order, which Dawn placed for both of them.

"Yes, your business was established a year ago and by all records has been a success from day one," she said.

"Oh good, you've done the basic homework."

"Always, Dawn. What kind of details do you have for me?"

Forty minutes and three coffees with cream, not milk, exactly two drops of vanilla syrup—not the fake stuff and a dollop of whipped cream later, Kari wanted to use every curse word she knew, so she would get fired. Not a sentence she spoke had been left uninterrupted. Her written notes had been scrutinized for precision and more than once a pinch of the scone that had been ordered for her had been eaten.

Even though she hadn't asked for the pastry, once she took a bite of it, Kari had been possessive. Then again, it was entirely possible that she was looking for get out of jail worthy reasons to break a plate over the woman's head. "It's going to cost you ten thousand dollars," Kari interrupted another tirade about the lackluster quality of wool these days.

"Fine, whatever," Dawn said with a dismissive wave of the hand. "But I need to have results within the month. I'm done here. I have a very important business meeting to go to. Anyhow, check in later, dear child. And the next time we meet, for the love of beauty, at least try to look presentable. Someone is bound to see you with me."

Kari sat in the booth stunned, until her phone rang. The meeting had gone even worse than she had imagined. However, asking for and getting a check for a fifty percent down payment had been an added bonus. If nothing else, she had five grand for enduring the meeting.

"We decided to go to a painting with vodka course," Kelli said.

"Wine," Kari corrected absently.

"Whatever, be home at six, so we can leave."

"She called me ugly," Kari said, still working it over in her mind.

"What? Who called you ugly?"
"My client, she just called me ugly."
"I'm so coming along with you, when you present her with her final bill and show her what you really look like," Kelli said with a snort. "I guess your skills have gotten better."

Kari hung up and tried to organize a plan. Despite being told she was unattractive, her brain still spun around the fact of the ten thousand dollar paycheck she was earning. She knew, in the end, it probably wasn't going to be enough for having to deal with the woman. She pulled a laptop out of her backpack and got ready to do some more research.

Using a pen and notepad had been one more trick she had learned. The lack of technology allowed people to relax just a bit more around her. The sight of a laptop apparently meant she would be looking up clients on the super-secret private detective website that gave up all their deepest, darkest secrets.

Frankly, she enjoyed using a journal and a pen; it relaxed her to write in longhand. Of course today's session with Dawn would make her rethink the practice. Everything from her handwriting to the actual notes she took had been under scrutiny. A smile spread over Kari's face. She'd made more money than she ever had before and, on top of it, she wasn't chasing a cheater. Maybe it would be so bad. At the very least, she wouldn't have to look at naked asses.

~~

Six hours later she closed her laptop and stretched with a huge sigh. Rather than moving to another spot, she'd stayed at the coffee shop to get the basic research done. She'd done a preliminary check in the ten minutes she'd had before the meeting, but her aim was to get as much information as possible.

Much to her frustration, it had been difficult to find out much else about Dawn or her business. In fact, Kari had to burn through four favors to get what should have been easy details about the woman and the business. Seemingly both Dawn and her business had just appeared out of the ether. In every avenue she had tried, there simply hadn't been a trace of the woman.

At least tracing the business had been easier, only because licenses were needed. Although the company was registered to Dawn, there had been an anonymous backer who had given her the loan. Kari knew it would be better to continue to work on it the next day because she didn't want any of her money to go to a new laptop after she smashed it in frustration. Wine and painting was sounding more attractive by the moment.

She packed up and was home in twenty minutes. The stop by the bank had proved fruitful as the check had cleared. The suite was quiet, meaning either her friends had left her or she'd beat them home. Either way it meant a long hot shower. She wasted no time in dumping her backpack on her bed and stripped as she walked to the bathroom. She was singing loudly in the shower when the door slammed open.

"Can you leave poor Tay-Tay's song alone? You're making it seem like a great idea for them to continue to ignore each other."

Kari grinned and sang louder. Being on key wasn't one of her talents, but she loved to give shower concerts nonetheless. She took an extra four minutes and twenty seconds, to sing the song over again. As she toweled dry, Red struck her head back in the door.

"Are you done assaulting my ears?"

"It's not like the original was any better. Anyhow I'm done. All yours wolf-bait."

"Wow, I can't wait to hear how your day went. Someone needs to tell FGM a house this big needs more than one shower."

Kari left the bathroom and carefully looked over her closet. Even though she generally made it a habit not to spend money before the clients had paid in full. The down payment check had cleared easily. She could definitely use a few more clothes to augment her wardrobe.

"Can I borrow your peasant blouse?" she called out to Mimi.

"Of course, just keep the damn thing. I haven't worn it since our big reveal. I don't know if I can actually wear it again."

Kari took her time dressing, after the many insults Dawn gave her, she needed to feel gorgeous. She wore the peasant blouse that showed her assets with an advantage of a scooped neckline. Her skirt was slim but not quite a pencil cut, because it wouldn't accommodate her very rounded ass.

She sat on the couch and tried to come up with a new plan. Her old ways of researching had failed her. Kari had just reconciled to having to make her way inside of the shipping yard, when her roommates came down the stairs.

They opted to walk since it was close and no one wanted to be the DD. The small town around the college was still in the growth phase, after a major industry change. Trendy and interesting businesses had cropped up; everything from restaurants to art studios to Indie bookstores.

The streets were brightly lit and despite being a Wednesday, plenty of foot traffic moved about. The women made it to the art studio with five minutes to spare. They took the front row of easels and waited for the instructor.

Kari looked up just in time to see FGM float into the room. She tried not to look sour, but she had been looking forward to a night of wine and possibly sexy-hot male instructor teaching them how to mix a palate of colors.

"Welcome to *Wine and Brushes*, Lovelies. Tonight we are going to sample great vintage wines and paint our dreams.

Prepare to let down barriers and embrace your inner most desires."

Kari nearly groaned out loud.

Here we go again.

A few hours later and her mind had been changed. Even though she had expected FGM to make the night awkward, instead the wine had been delicious and Kari was proud of her painting. They had been guided to create an evening picnic under a full moon. Red had included a small wolf in the shadows, causing much eye rolling. Otherwise they'd had a great time.

~~

Two weeks later found Kari watching the docks. The smell of brackish water wouldn't leave her nose and the grime under her nails kept layering on. Still, she'd learned a good cup of hot coffee, especially in November, was valid currency.

Emil, the security officer, had proudly told her all about his job. He boasted about how he patrolled the facility on foot, where his lazy coworkers always used a vehicle. Also he was the only one who routinely and monitored the closed circuit television systems, alarms and "other very important facility systems."

He reminded Kari of a shorter, rounder version of a mall Santa, especially because he laughed all the time. He'd also regretfully denied her a tour of the shipyard. She doubted he'd believed her cover as an aspiring author, writing about haunted shipyard, but it didn't matter, she'd already learned the schedule of security movement.

After promising to make Red two dozen truffles, she'd gotten a shipping manifest from one of Dawn's recent shipments. She had ordered hundreds of spinning wheels, spindles, treadles, and Charkhas for her antiques company from India and Russia. Kari had no idea who would steal the merchandise, nor why. The hacked delivery manifests also showed for each shipment, only one crate of the antiques had been stolen. Maybe a gang of rouge senior citizens were feeling feisty?

The thought made her giggle. Then again, it was day six of her stake out and she was tired of watching forklifts moving containers around. She shifted from foot to foot. The nights had been getting progressively much cooler.

Her roommates had kept her company via snarky texts. All cat based of course. Kari had been tempted to send them a selfie of her butt, but refused to sink that low. And of course she knew Red might be tempted to make a special website dedicated to her ample asset.

Her peripheral vision caught a figure moving from shadow to shadow. She watched it move and she stomach started to tingle. It headed directly towards Dawn's lots and containers. She leaned forward to force blood into her toes, in case she had to move quickly. Tripping over her feet would never be lived down.

The person in the shadows stopped in front of Dawn's container, but did nothing else. Kari wanted to scream as he walked away. She'd gotten a break as the man stopped under a light to read a small piece of paper. A map she'd guessed. His raven black hair and sharp beak of a nose only helped to make him look dangerous. She shivered and pulled in to make herself smaller and more invisible. The man looked all around the container, walking around it four times before leaving.

The next few nights were the same routine. He never broke into the container, just paced around it. Kari had examined the containers after he left each night, but there was nothing special about them, nor did he leave any evidence behind. She needed something soon, because Dawn's month deadline drew close.

A clear moonless night, forty-eight hours later, found Kari racing around shipping containers back toward the city. She ignored the stitch of pain in her side. If she stopped she wasn't sure she would live to get the information she'd learned back to her friends. With only two days left, she'd finally gotten her answers. The last shipment had been broken into by Crow-man and after he'd cracked open the crate and grabbed a few pieces he'd run. And during his mad dash out of the shipping yard, he'd dropped one of the pieces he had stolen. Kari scooped it up. She pocketed the item before she could examine it because someone had started to chase her. She focused on the gate a few hundred feet in front of her and pushed herself harder.

At least I wore my work boots. Oh, yes. I've got this…

She got to the gate, grabbed it to slip through and felt a sharp prick in her thigh. Looking down she saw the end of a small dart.

"Are you kidding me?" she muttered.

She plucked the offending object out of her leg and tossed it aside. The drug in her system worked quickly and she began to wobble. The world went into Technicolor swirls and she fell forward and into darkness.

When Kari woke, she found herself in the dark and lying on a blow up mattress. A pungent scent surrounded her and seemed to steal away what air she could breathe. She tried to take a deep breath to clear her head. The inhaled scent caused her to lapse into a coughing fit, as it overwhelmed her. She figured it probably was from the sedative coursing through her system, but it still made her gag. She forced herself to sit up.

She looked around, trying to get her bearings. Instead a rush of images passed through her head. Her, as Puss, talking with a man and then the man flailing in the water. The moment she convinced a group of people to raise her friend to level of hero. Her shifting from cat to fairy to observe her work and call it good. Each version of herself showed her to be cunning, light on her feet, and a survivor. She worked to help those she loved, and she wasn't about to change that.

"Well, good, you're awake."

She squinted up at the man in front of her and swallowed a gasp. It wasn't the guy who looked like a crow who stood before her, but instead a man so beautiful she had no words. She was just proud not to be drooling.

"I just need to know why such a pretty woman spent the last few weeks skulking around the dirty ship yard. Imagine my surprise when Emil turned you in. You flirted with him and everything. I know you didn't steal from the container, so why just watch as it was robbed?"

Kari watched him walk around the room. His muscles rippled against the satiny fabric covering him from waist to ankle. He sat in a chair and she made eye contact with him again.

"Who are you?" she asked, proud her voice came out strong.

"Dib, and who are you?"

"Kari. A private detective, but you already know that, right?"

The man smiled as he nodded.

"Why did you let the man steal?"
"Well, I'm not the police. And before I got chased, I had planned to follow him home and get the information I needed for my client."

Dib pulled out the small golden spinning wheel. He spun the wheel. Kari watched it go around and around willing her brain make sense of the fragments. She must have missed something, not all the pieces were adding up.

"Why are you interested in a container that belongs to someone else? Why do you ever care about these antiques?"

"Let me share a few things with you. Help you make sense of the bits and pieces you have already figured out. My employer needed a particular antique, but couldn't allow it to be traced back to them. Enter Dawn, lovely, vain and not the most observant person in the world. However, she is great at finding antiques. Now that we've found what we've needed, no more of her crates will be tampered with."

"And now, you're going to kill me?"

"Why would I do that?"

Kari stared at him and wondered if this was when FGM would come to the rescue. Then again, in all of her histories, she had been the savior. She wasn't tied up, just woozy from the drug still in her system. There was still a chance for her.

"You just told me your plan."

"I didn't tell you the best part, yet."

"Which is what?"

"Inhale, sweet one."

Dib held a vial under her nose. Kari tried and failed not to breathe. The heady scent of gardenia enveloped her. She felt relaxed and calm.

"The spinning wheel is magical and part of the greater plan. It pulls your soul into another realm—it looks like a deep slumber, just like in the stories. What better person to find it, than the person it was originally used on? I know you and your friends thought you were the only fairy tale creatures that had been woken. You're not. In fact, there will more changes happening for the better. This world is about to change."

Kari tried to move but couldn't. She sat on the mattress and willed her legs to move. For a tale known to be a cat, she sure had succumbed to the curiosity aspect. She watched as Dib leaned in close.

"I can't have you running back and spilling all this news, so you're going to have to come with me. Don't worry about your soul; this device is already destined for another."

He covered her mouth and nose with a handkerchief. Kari slowly slumped forward and her eyes fluttered closed.

I hope I have nine lives

Her last thought melted away and she knew nothing else.

Smoke and Mirrors

Kelli looked in her rearview mirror sighed in disgust. It'd been a long time since she'd fumbled a crack on the first try. Ever since she was a little girl, she'd always been able to feel each tick and tumbler. All the craziness going on had them all on edge. FGM had told them to expect weird events, but it hadn't prepared them enough.

Kari had been missing for a week. FGM hadn't responded to their calls. The visit to the police had yielded nothing. The feeling or urgency wound its way up into her brain and didn't let go. She, Red, and Mimi were on alert, but they didn't know for what. The tension kept rolling in. It suddenly went from cute fairy tales, to impending danger.

Even still, she wasn't used to failing a safe crack and she didn't plan to give up the most challenge lock she'd ever faced. Exhaling a deep breath, she pushed open the car door and stood up. She tugged her skirt into place and ran her fingers through her short spiky do. She still couldn't believe her roommates had talked her into a haircut.

"Break the stereotype," she muttered. "No one warned me about not having hair to twirl around my fingers when I'm nervous."

Kelli opened the door to the building and back to the suite where her greatest failure had taken place twenty minutes prior. Without hesitation, she knocked on the door and sighed in relief as it was pulled open a few seconds later.

"Oh, you're back."

A petite woman smiled at her and pushed the door open wide. She didn't seem upset at all, and which gave Kelli hope.

"Yes. I'm very sorry about the upset from before, but I've had a long week. It's no excuse, I know. If you're willing to give me another try, I can open your safe."

"Well, that sounds good to me. Besides, I really don't know where I could get another safe crack at such late notice, anyhow. Come on in. What do you think went wrong last time?"

"I don't know. Well, maybe I do. I've only ever dreamed about the Trill 07 Safe. I suppose I got too excited," Kelli said. "However, I also know I won't fail you twice."

"Of course you won't. Come on in. Do you want some tea?"

She looked at the young woman standing across the desk from her and tried not to stare. She knew in the pit of her gut she looked at Snow White. Ebony black hair, huge brown eyes, porcelain white skin and naturally bright red lips. She was dainty, tiny, and had all the assets a princess would have from popular media descriptions. As Kelli stared, Snow smiled and tilted her head, just so. The young woman kept her eye contact until Kelli fidgeted.

"May I ask you a question?"

"Of course."

"I feel silly, since you're my client. But I didn't get a chance to ask your name, due to my fumble. All your work ticket gave me was Ms. S."

"Ms. Schnee. It's German, in case you wanted to know. I decided when I was going to start my own business that I would need a new name to go with my new venture. Ms. White is just so common, don't you think?"

Kelli nodded and worked her best to keep her face passive. The woman looked pleased with herself. She had decided to stick with the original, but with a twist. One of the first things she and her roommates had done, once they learned about their fairy tale roots, was explore them. Hundreds upon hundreds of variations of her own tale existed and she had read them all. She could only imagine how many version of Snow White existed; after all, it had been turned into a beloved movie.

After all of her research, she didn't find it coincidental at all that she would end up finding another person who had been awoken. Even less surprise that it would be Snow White, considering how similar their stories tropes were. Kelli also learned in her story, the original version, she hadn't been some bratty child, but instead an old woman. A mean one with a foul mouth and described as ugly. She thanked Joseph Cundall, for making her a cute little girl, on a daily basis.

"Of course," Kelli murmured. "Should I go ahead and get started?"

"Yes, yes. Of course you can. The safe needs to be open and the code I need wasn't delivered as promised. It's holding up my next plan of action, so get on with it."

The high-pitched chipper voice made shivers run up Kelli's spine. She could just imagine her client frolicking through the woods and singing to animals. It was too perfect, light and airy. And followed her.

"Do you mind if I ask how you came to have a safe you don't know the combination to?" she asked her client.

"Well, Lyall knew I would need a safe to store all of my documents. I have some new upcoming ventures and expansions which are all very exciting. Anyhow the safe had been delivered before I expected it. An envoy was supposed to show up the next day with an important envelope, but he never showed. I've reached out to Lyall, but there's been no answer, although I know he's an incredibly busy man. He's very important. But I'm not too worried. He's planned everything for me and so far it's worked out perfectly. He's always helped me with what I need to do. I mean, if not for him, I wouldn't even have this business," Ms. Schnee said, her lyrical rambling on. "Anyhow, you know the way."

Kelli walked quickly toward the office that held the safe. She knew the only reason she had really botched the job, was the woman walking briskly next to her. The job had come through the usual contact form from her website. There had been noting to warn her it had come from a fairy tale princess who skipped into the room next to her. With a bird on her shoulder no less. Granted it was a golden brooch, but still a bird.

Kelli followed her through the suite, back into the small office where the safe dominated the back of the room. She took a deep breath and calmed herself. She blew a nervous breath through her teeth. Her phone rang and she dropped her chalk. She watched it shatter into small pieces and then looked down at her phone.

"Sorry, I need to take this call."

Ms. Schnee smiled and nodded her head. Kelli walked calmly out of the office, out to her jeep, and sat. After locking the doors, she called her roommates back.

"Please tell me this is important," she said. "I need to finish this job."

"Kari's cell phone was found at the shipyards," Red said. "The police asked me to come down and identify it."

"We knew she was working there, this isn't new information," Kelli said. "And they asked you to ID a phone?"

"Yes, they did. I took the SD card out of the back. Aside from a sickening array of photos from the club meant to blackmail us; there is a memo file."

Kelli drummed her fingertips against the steering wheel.

"Are you pausing for dramatic effect? Can I get the rest of the details, Red?"

"Patience, Clepto. The file is encrypted and I haven't been able to break it. I just paused to enter another line of code."

The drumming against the wheel got faster. Red had never failed a hack. Just like she had never failed a crack. Kelli looked around, noting idly how the parking lot lampposts resembled gnarled branches of trees. Small bronze bird statues adorned them.

"I'm working for Snow White," she blurted out.

Of all the reactions, Kelli hadn't expected her roommate to lose her mind and laugh uncontrollably. She listened to the hysteria while watching the lights flicker on. She sighed, hating how early it got dark in November.

"Well, you're being useless. I need to get back and open the safe. Let me know when you make progress."

She hung up the phone, a lump forming in her throat. She shook her head to get over the rising well of emotions. Swirls of information flashed through her mind. Her own pasts mingled and played like snippets of a movie. She never wanted to see a bowl of oatmeal again in her life.

She walked back into the office and strode into the room without breaking her stride. She held up her hand to stop the questions Snow had poised on her cherry red lips. Kelli stopped in front of the safe and smiled. She ignored the pout; and reached for the dial.

"Are you in college?"

The question startled Kelli and she turned to face her client.

"Yes."

She waited for Snow to say more, but was waved back to the safe as the woman said nothing more. Rubbing her hands against her pant legs, she tuned back to face the safe. She turned the dial slowly. It stuttered a tiny bit. 18. With a smile, she wrote down the number and turned the dial again.

"Do you have a boyfriend?"

"What?"

Kelli turned around and stared at the woman. The first time around, it had just been a barrage of inane chatter. She had gotten so distracted, she couldn't think. Especially when the songs started. The wide brown eyes were friendly.

"Do you have a boyfriend?"

"What does this have to do with cracking your safe?"

"Oh nothing. Lyall told me I needed to practice my small chat. I prefer to talk to my pets. I guess sometimes I say the wrong things."

Kelli faced the safe again, just in case she gave in and laughed. However, it did strike her that her client knew she was Snow White. All of a sudden she wanted to know how, but she didn't have any idea how to broach the subject.

"Is Lyall your boyfriend?"

"Oh, I wish."

The breathy sigh was just what Kelli imagined would come from the princess. Apparently some stereotypes were true.

"No Lyall is my benefactor."

Now the pause was Kelli's. She began turning the dial again. It bought her the precious time she needed to compose herself. It ticket at 12 and she wrote down the next number.

"I'm sorry; I don't know what a benefactor is."

A light giggle filled the room.

"Well the way you say it, makes him sound like my pimp."

Kelli tried not to swallow her tongue in shock. Snow White shouldn't ever say the word pimp.

"No, no, no, no. I mean. Wow, you said the word…," she said as the blush heated up her face. "So, what is a benefactor?"

"You're only charging me to open the safe and not by the hour, yes?"

Kelli smiled and nodded.

"Okay, I've always wanted a girlfriend to share stories with. Come sit with me. There is a lot to tell."

After waiting a few moments, just in case her client broke into song, Kelli sat.

"This all started in June, I can't believe everything has happened so fast. So anyhow, I graduated in June, and unlike everyone else, I didn't want to go to college. My dream was to open an exotic pet shop, but I didn't have the money. I went to work in a daycare," the woman gave a shudder. "Thanks to my mean step-mama, I had to get a job. I found out, I don't do well with little people. They are just so…so messy. And little. And needy."

Kelli wished she had a tape recorder; and some popcorn. Snow's eyes sparkled as she got into telling her tale.

"Well, my plans were falling apart because I had no way to open my little exotic pet shop. I decided that instead I would just get married or at the very least find myself a good sugar daddy," Snow said and then leaned in close. "I was just worried I would attract some old grizzled fatty mcbutterpants."

The urge to grab her cell phone and tape the conversation made Kelli's palms itch. She couldn't believe the amazing conversation would only ever exist between her, Snow, and the wall.

"Anyhow, I started looking around on these dating sites. To be fair, I'm pretty terrible with a computer. Clean a house? I'm your girl. Figure out how to navigate a website and I'm lost. Well, fortunately, Lyall, contacted me before any old gross man did."

Snow turned and dug through a purse at her side. After a few moments, she pulled out a piece of paper and thrust it toward Kelli. It was the insert from a photo frame showing a smiling man with wide brown eyes and dark hair.

"But this is from a picture frame…"

"Of course it is, but it's how he described himself. I wanted to have a picture, so this is the closest thing I could get."

"You've never met Lyall?"

"No, but I will soon. He told me a few weeks ago that once his business is done, we will get together and celebrate his success."

"Do you know what his business is?"

"Nope, but I'll know when he tells me."

Kelli doubted she could ever be blindly optimistic as Snow. Meeting guys online was risky, especially guys like this Lyall person, who seemingly helped out just because.

"Lyall seems almost too good to be true."

"He's wonderful," Snow gushed. "He helped me set up my own business. Even better, he showed me how to be assertive. For years I was terrorized by my step-mother, can you believe that little twist stayed in this life? She used to call me ugly and mocked me for loving my pets. Why I ever stayed with that c…"

"Whoa!" Kelli interrupted. "Name calling is a bit harsh don't you think?"

"Well, she wasn't very nice," Snow said with a grin. "Wow, girl chat is fun, but enough chatter. I need my safe open still."

Kelli nodded went back to the safe. After a few flicks of the dial the last number, 53, and the tumblers dropped. She was disappointed. The safe had been on the top of her list for a few years. It seemed too easy only using three numbers. Out of the corner of her eye, she saw Snow jumping up and down and clapping.

"Thank you. You're the best friend I've ever had. I hate to be rude, but here's your check."

The piece of paper was pushed into her hand and she was waved toward the door. Kelli walked out with a shake of her head and walked back to her jeep. She really wanted to know what the safe held, but had no chance as Snow hadn't let her open the door.

She drove back to the house ready for a glass of wine and a long hot bath. She parked in the drive and as she walked to the porch saw FGM sitting on the porch swing.

"Isn't it a beautiful night?

"It's forty degrees," Kelli said. "And you're in a sleeveless dress."

"I'm a fairy; the wings and glitter keeps me warm."

"I don't see wings," she snorted. "Why haven't you responded to our calls? Kari is missing."

FGM nodded and patted the seat next to her. Kelli sat, letting the motion soothe her. She noticed the air did feel warmer on the swing. They rocked for a while in silence.

"I didn't ignore you on purpose. First of all, time moves differently in other realms. I've only been gone thee nights as far as I'm concerned. Second, I don't know where Kari is."

"But you're our fairy godmother," Kelli protested. "Shouldn't you know everything about us?"

The swing stopped.

"No. I'm *a* fairy godmother, but not yours. There is another for me to find. You all are the heroes in this world. I wish I could help you all find Kari, but I have no way to."

"What do you mean? Can't you use your magic? All we have are a bunch of old stories stuffed up in our heads. Which by the way is some crap," Kelli said. "You have to find some better way to awaken people. It's not fair to be letting loose into the battlefields and only have a bunch of memories of a million tales as the only weapon. And the whole flooding the mind thing? It's a rush, and not in a good way."

The rocking started again. They sat in silence looking up at the stars.

"Believe it or not, I'm in new territory here too. Your world doesn't believe much in magic. Instead of embracing what's special, people focus on what they can amass. Part of the reasons we even have fairy tales are to teach people. But instead of reading a book, most of your world stares at a phone screen."

Kelli was surprised at the hard edge to FGM's voice. She thought she might have imagined it, but when she looked at the fairy, her lips were pressed into a thin tight line. Nothing would be gained by complaining and whining. So, she just rocked.

The door opened and broke her trance. She looked over and saw Red and Mimi standing.

"It's a bit chilly, don't cha think?"

"I was just talking to FGM."

Kelli rolled her eyes in exasperation as she looked around to find the swing empty.

"Apparently she left me to tell you all the bad news. She can't find Kari. She's not our fairy godmother and we're going to have to do this on our own."

The swing dipped as Red and Mimi sat on either side of her. The rocking motion became soothing again.

"I guess we need to make a plan," Mimi said. "Things always look easier with a plan."

The girls sat on the swing until yawns punctuated their conversation. Kelli tossed and turned for a few hours in her bed, and eventually got up when sun light spilled into her bedroom. She tried to think through her story lines. The use of three was big: chairs, beds, and bowls. Finding the fit seemed to be important. Although Kelli did wonder why the baby stuff won out; she figured the Mama's stuff would've made more sense, since the middle position.

"Apparently being a golden haired lock pick is all I've got."

Her brain clicked and she smiled. A plan began to form. She got up and made the coffee. Fairy tale women or not, Mimi was downright nasty before coffee hit her system.

Kelli checked her phone for the millionth time to make sure she still had a connection. She pushed a button once and smiled when two tones came back a few second later. Red sat in her jeep a few blocks away. Once she got the signal they would swoop in and provide the getaway.

She ran her hands through her short hair again. She hoped she hadn't pissed off the fairy tale gods of luck by getting rid of her defining characteristic. Kelli exhaled harshly, trying to get rid of the nervousness. The plan was simple, but everyone had to do their part.

Snow left the building and like planned Mimi intercepted her with a kitten. It was a beautiful fluffy white, with golden eyes and a bandaged paw. As anticipated, Snow crooned and made soft noises to the kitten. Mimi asked for help and a ride to the veterinarian, on the opposite side of town which would buy Kelli the time she needed.

As soon as the women left Kelli walked back to the building with no problems. She went up to the flights of steps to where Snow's office was and easily picked the door lock. The lights were off, so she stood still in the darkness to let her eyes adjust. She made it back to the rear office.

Snow had shut the safe before leaving but Kelli knew the combination. 18-12-53. The door swung open and she gasped.

"No way," she breathed.

Before her, suspended on hooks in the safe, was a mirror. *The* mirror from Snow's story, at least she guessed so, because the surface swirled and roiled with what looked like smoke, beneath the surface. She stood mesmerized by the movement and fluctuating colors.

Kelli startled out of her trance as her phone beeped. Red asked for an update. She shook her head, grateful for the interference and got back to the mission. Above the mirror was a shelf with several envelopes. She hoped one of them would have the clues they needed. While she and the others couldn't be sure her case and Kari's were involved in any way, it only made sense they would be. If not, they would err on the side of caution and act like they were.

The first envelope held contracts. To Kelli's shock, Snow owned the entire seven floored building. The next envelopes were business licenses; all of them involved with various pet pampering plans in place. The next one held blueprint plans. She got more frustrated with each one she opened.

"Seriously? There's nothing more than her plans to have her exotic pet village in this building?" Kelli asked the air. "How am I supposed to find out what is going on?"

"You just need to ask the proper question."

Kelli shirked and whirled around—and saw nothing.

"Who's there?" she called out.

"Me."

The words sounded from behind her and again she spun. And saw the face in the mirror. He took her breath with how perfect his face was. Golden wavy hair, storm gray eyes and lips she could almost feel on her own.

"How… what… oh my goodness," she said. "How is it even possible?"
"Why do people bother to ask who's there if they're going to be surprised to get an answer?"

"You're the magic mirror," Kelli squeaked.

"And you cut your hair."

"You know me?"

"Goldilocks, of course. You've grown into a beauty," The Mirror said.

"Why does Snow need you?" Kelli asked after a few moments of open mouth nothingness.

"I serve a very important function. I don't only tell people who the gorgeous ones are. I'm made of magic."

"But magic doesn't work here," she protested. "How are you even possible?"

"You didn't listen very carefully, now did you? FGM told you magic doesn't work very well here. But it definitely works, even though when it does most people deny what they saw," The Mirror said.

Kelli paused while she took in the information. The gorgeous vision captivated her a few moments more.

"What kind of magic do you have?"

"The old kind," the face in the mirror winked at her.

"Why were you brought here?" she asked.

"You're quick to catch on. I am needed to act as a bridge between the realms. During the next solstice the borders between this realm and another are thin enough for others to pass through."

"How can people cross the realms? Aren't we tied to where we come from?"

"You ask such refreshing questions. Snow White had about a million questions about animals, her looks and if her step-mother wanted her dead," The Mirror said. "And I do mean almost a million questions about animals. She really needs to find her Prince."

Kelli snorted in laughter.

"Being tied to your realm isn't quite true. If you are clever enough, there are ways to travel between the realms. The more difficult part is finding a way to anchor yourself," he explained.

"What is a way that would work between my realm and the other?"

"Information transfer is the easiest way."

"Wow."

Kelli let the information mull around in her brain for a moment.

"Tell me more," she said.

The face in the mirror winked at her. Part of her regretted him only having a face.

"Well?" she asked after moments of silence.

"You have to play by the rules," he said with a smile.

"Oh, okay," she said. "Who is behind this all? Do you know where Kari is? How is her case involved with this one? How can we defeat the bad guy?"

"Well now, we can't just go and give you all the secrets."

The voice sounded from behind her, and with a sigh Kelli turned around. The man standing in the room behind her made her stare. He was tall, dark hair, darker eyes and she actually wanted to touch him to see if the muscles under his shirt were real.

"Holy wow, are all of you fairy tale men, gorgeous?"

"Yes," The Mirror said with a chuckle.

"Despite the lovely chat you had with our friend here, you can't actually know everything that's going to happen."

Kelli tried to gauge if she could actually make it out of the office.

"Nope," The Mirror said.

"I didn't ask anything, did I?" she hissed.

"Magic," he countered.

"The good news for you is you will be reunited with your friend," the dark haired man said.

"She's not dead?"

"What kind of men have you two dated? I'm not an animal," the man said. "But I can't you have following me and ruining the plans, no matter how cute you are."

Kelli blushed and then got aggravated with herself for doing so. And then more so, when the dark haired man, pushed her hair away from her face.

"Can I at least know your name, since you're going to kidnap me?"

"It's Dib. Oh, and don't worry about your friends. I already sent a signal to their phones and they expect to meet you at home."

Kelli felt his smile all the way down in her stomach. And then he blew into his hand and a cloud of powder in her face. The world went hazy and then dark.

A brother in need

"Mimi, you have to help me."

Mimi smiled into the phone at the over exuberant voice coming from her brother. He always had a plan, but often got disappointed when things fell through. The difference was that this time, things had gone right. Very right.

Once she learned about being Gretel from the fairy tales, her life actually made more sense. She had Harvey had been orphaned at a young age. They had stayed with one foster mother, who had starved them. Another family tried to sell them off, and after that debacle, she'd requested they be left in the care of the state at a group home.

Being older meant Mimi always had taken charge and Harvey relied on her, for everything. Usually it meant getting him out of trouble financially. Every time something new and shiny came out, he had to have it. This meant his apartment housed any and all of the newest technology available, and an empty fridge.

Mimi knew her brother wanted all the flash and glamor. She thought she wanted quiet stability, but after all the craziness she had experienced with her roommates missing, she'd started to rethink her options. After thinking hard about what her life could be, she yearned to visit faraway lands and see new cultures. She wanted to find her true purpose and have adventures.

"Are you even listening to me?" Harvey's question broke into her thoughts.

"Sorry, Harve. I'm trying to figure out how I'm supposed to help you with this particular situation. You're going on a date," Mimi grinned. "I'm not going to be the third wheel to help you talk to her."

In addition to buying things on a whim, Harvey had declared himself an innovative inventor. He just knew for certain that his next phone app would be the one to make him rich. Finally, after fifty failures, he had done it. While his idea wasn't new, it was a dating app, his app was smarter. Not only did the app set up random blind dates at the newest trendy place in the city. The best part of the program was it set up for a friend to be on an autodial with a timer set for twenty minutes. If the date was going well, the daters could enter a cancel code; if it the date sucked, their friends would show up and save them.

Mimi shook her head. The app had become instantly popular. People loved the rescue feature and it was downloaded thousands of times each hour. The idea had been hers, but the coding skills were all his. She, of course, didn't mind him taking all the credit.

While Harvey enjoyed the unfettered success, he hadn't expected, having to go on a date of his own. During an interview with the local television station Harvey was asked to show how the app worked. After filling out the basic profile, his phone buzzed to let him know a date had been set. And because he was on television, he had been coerced into going through with it.

The date was a smashing success, and ever since Mimi had gotten at least three calls every day. Either Harvey panicked when the app did well and also when the app downloads slowed down. He reached out to ask her if she had any new ideas for apps, because his fans were asking about it. And he called before every single date with Mary. All four of them.

Mimi shrugged, at least she heard from him all the time. After Kari and Kelli had gone missing with no traces, she couldn't bear the thought of losing anyone else. The women had become close, they were much more than just roommates; they were true friends. Red was just as nervous, but didn't say anything.

FGM had been gone again, and even though she knew time moved differently between the realms, it was hard being out of contact. Her friends were missing. Something bad was coming and they had no way to plan for it because whatever the other two had found out had disappeared with them. It made her feel alone, and Mimi learned it was a feeling she despised. With a few well-placed non-committal sounds to Harvey, she quickly said good-bye and hung up.

All was calm and quiet until the day after Thanksgiving. As she and Red sat watching movies and eating popcorn. They were on their fourth bowl with no shame. The phone rang and Red gave Mimi a grin.

"Bet Harvey can't figure out if his underwear is on correctly."
"Ewww, stop it. I'm sure he's just trying to figure out if he should give her a gift on their fifth date or wait until the sixth."

"You need to stop coddling that boy and let him make some of his own decisions," Red scoffed.

"Easier said than done. He's family and family is everything," Mimi said.

"Well when I get a family, I'll remember that."

Mimi picked up the phone; the words to advise him to pick the green shirt were on her lips, when he interrupted her in a panic.

"Mary is missing," Harvey said. "She won't answer my calls and no one has seen her."

"Slow down, give me the details," Mimi said. She tried to project calm even though she was on alert.

She listened as Harvey told her about the contest Mary had entered. A new etiquette school announced a new class and would choose twenty entrants who would win a scholarship. It was all inclusive and promised to transform anyone in just a week.

Mary had won and left for the course. Harvey hadn't heard anything since and called her.

"It's only been four days?" she asked.

"Yes, but Mary and I talk each morning and night," he said.

"Do you think there were rules about outside contact?"

"No. She promised to keep our contact. When she started she was excited. When I talked to her last, she sounded different, and then she stopped calling and picking up."

Mimi sighed softly. She figured the school had some strict rules about outside contact.

"And it's not there anymore."

Those words got her attention.

"What's not there?'

"The finishing school. I dropped her off for her first day, so I could see it. It used to be right next to the tea shop we loved so much. I went this morning to go find her and it's gone."

"I'm on my way."

Mimi hung up and went to his apartment. They went to the location and found it empty. After calling Red, the three began to scour the city for any trace of the school. Even though Harvey told them twenty women had been accepted, no one else seemed to notice anyone else missing.

Red muttered under her breath about more fairy tale crap as they walked in the frigid air. Harvey looked scared and Mimi had no ideas. For another week, success eluded them. Again FGM was nowhere to be seen.

"I think I have something."

The loud voice on her phone at six am made Mimi curse.

"You don't have to speak, just listen. A new ad was just bought for my app," Harvey said. "It's a week-long workshop for women to release their inner princess. Only the most lovely will be accepted. You have to go sign up."

Mimi grumbled.

"Okay, I tweaked your application and you were accepted. I'll text the directions to you."

She stumbled out of bed and made it to the kitchen. She slapped at the buttons until the coffee machine came on. After two mugs of coffee, Harvey's phone call sunk into her brain.

"I'm going to princess school? You've got to be kidding me."

The next day found her sitting on a plush velvet chair. While it looked gorgeous, it had a hard seat, and forced Mimi to sit very upright. Only one other woman sat next to her.

"Did you get into the course too?" Mimi asked, leaning over to talk to the young woman. "Because I don't know if I'm in the right place. I expected there to be more of us."

The young woman turned to look at Mimi, breathing a bit quickly. She had wide hazel eyes, amazing cheekbones and hair pulled back into a bun. Mimi felt plain just sitting next to the woman. Maybe she should've dressed up more. She had no idea how she would be able to convince the head mistress to accept her. Her brother had tweaked the electronic application, but being seen in person might not work.

"This is the right place. Although I'm not sure how you even got invited. At most you're pretty, not stunning or gorgeous. You should probably leave and save yourself the embarrassment."

Mimi put down her coffee and fixed a glare at the young woman. She stood up and got ready to give her a piece of her mind. A far door opened and a tall poised woman came out.

"Ladies it's so wonderful to see you. I'm Ella, CEO of Positive Self Images. Tatiana, you can go in and join the posture course; you evidently still need some work. And Mimi, you can come with me."

Mimi smiled softly; at least her posture didn't need work.

"You are lovely and already have grace. Why did you sign up?"

"I'm Mimi. I'm getting married in six months. Everyone tells me you're the best. I need to look and act perfect. If my mother-in-law isn't impressed, I might not be able to marry the love of my life."

Mimi tried to look hopeful and impressionable. Ella clasped her hands over her chest and cooed.

"A love story. I'm such a sucker for true love. Don't worry my dear. If a mouse can become a horse, I can certainly teach you to impress your new mama."

Mimi took a deep breath and pasted a wide smile on her face.

"I'm so glad you will help me. I only have one chance to make a good impression. I need to be as royal as possible," she pursed her lips.

Ella linked her arm through Mimi's and began walking down a long hall. Mimi walked quickly with the woman and tried to pay attention as instructions were rattled in her direction. There were so many classes to cram into the next two weeks, and she wasn't sure if she would survive being undercover.

"By the time you are done, you will be able to dance at any formal function and not stumble. You will be able to eat a seven course meal using the proper utensils, and you will look amazing all the time."

It sounded like two weeks of torture just to be pretty. Mimi's goal in life was to be an accountant. Numbers were consistent and quiet. She had already told Harvey that she would be moving to Kentucky to attend graduate school. Thankfully, because of Mary, he had no plans to follow her. For the first time in her life, she would only be responsible for herself.

After finishing some standard paperwork, she was given two hours to get her supplies and return. She went home and told Red about the good news.

"You're going to learn to eat a seven course meal and this is going to help us how?" Red asked, not even trying to hold back the laughter.

Mimi folded her jacket, shirt, and slacks up carefully into a small bag. As she had never gone camping, she had no idea of what to pack. Not to mention since it was for etiquette classes, everything needed to be dressy. She took a deep breath, trying not to hyperventilate as Red watched her.

"I'm not sure yet. Everything that's happened so far is scattered. We don't know what Kari found out at the docks. We have no idea what Kelli found in the safe. Apparently I will find something in this school, and I want to keep you updated. My plan to is to keep checking in," she said as she packed.

"Well Kelli sent us that message to meet at home and never showed," Red reminded her.

"Well, I'll call every chance I get. Now where is my bug spray?"

When she returned to the building there was a letter left for her on the chair she had been sitting on. The silence unnerved her. Only two hours prior, the place had been filled with music and other background noise.

She got back into Kelli's jeep and began to drive. She hoped her roommate wouldn't mind, no one else had a vehicle. Mimi tried not to shriek when FGM appeared in her peripheral vision. A small shower of glittered covered the dashboard.

"Why is there always glitter? This is never going to come out of the seats," she moaned.

"I got your messages just now and wanted to talk to you before you entered that place."

"That sounds ominous," Mimi muttered. "Can't you come with me? Don't you have a tie to Mary or something?"

"Not any more. I'm not sure how she's being hidden from me," FGM said.

"Can't you just materialize there, like you do with us?"

"No. In fact, once you park, I'll have to leave."

Mimi felt a jolt of panic. She didn't know where and how this would all end.

"It's just up the road a few miles. Turn off at Poplar Street and drive until you see the lot. You'll have to park and walk back through the forest," FGM guided her. "The finishing cabins are back a few miles. Bring flowers. Don't expect to be safe there."

"I don't expect to be safe anywhere," Mimi said, bristling a little bit. "And why bring flowers? I'm trying to find a kidnapped girl, not woo Ella. Are you sure the woods will keep you out?"

FGM shook her head with a small smile.

"Flowers were in the small print of the contract you signed. And no, I can't come with you."

"But you're Mary's fairy godmother. You've supposed to save her you know."

"No, I'm not. At least not from this. Each of you has been sent on a quest to help put together pieces of what will happen. With Kari and Kelli missing, I'm not sure if we will be able to figure it all out in time."

Mimi sighed in dejection.

"Thank you for the information. I'm not sure how Mary fits into all of this. I don't see how Ella's camp leads to missing girls either. But I will do what I always do, and help my brother."

"Here's hoping you won't wish you hadn't met me. Someday, when everything is all done, I hope we will all be able to sit down and have a good glass of wine and laugh about it all."

Mimi stared at FGM down for a long minute, neither of them blinking, and then squared her shoulders. She had girl to find, clues to figure out, and roommates to rescue. And to do that, she had to go camping.

Mimi walked carefully down a dirt path. It was sunlit, beautiful, and every little sound made her jump. After her memories came in, she understood why she had a fear of the forest. But camping… she just had no idea why people wanted to leave the comforts of air conditioning and a microwave. Cooking over a fire in bug infested cabins in humid weather, made no sense to her.

She panted lightly as she pulled her two cases toward her cabin. She looked at the bouquet of flowers making sure none of the greenery had fallen out. FGM had done her the solid of making them appear. Confident they were secure with their thorns pointed outward, she grunted as she continued to walk. Did Ella really expect all of her protégées to walk through the woods in heels? When she found a wilted pile— all daisies, of course— she stopped, dropped the fresh lavender colored roses on top of the wrinkled white flowers, and allowed her mouth curl into a broad smile.

Mimi sat down on the bed in the cabin and shook her head. While the campground looked rustic, the interior of the cabin was posh. A queen sized bed with satin sheets. Gleaming hard wood floors, interior plumbing and a cozy fireplace, finished the look.

"I could get used to camping like this," she said. "This might not even be bad."

A bell began to ring. According the instructional folder, it was time for evening dinner. As Mimi made it down she saw foil packets on the campfire. The smell was amazing and she couldn't wait to eat.

She left her cabin and walked, carefully, toward the fire. Mimi loved heels, but walking through the woods in them meant tiny measured steps, so she wouldn't fall.

"Welcome to camp," Ella said. "Tonight we are going to find the most deserving of you all."

A gong sounded and Ella turned and walked down a path. The group of young women, about ten in all, followed her. Thankfully it was a short trip. As Mimi made it through the clearing she saw a long formal table on a dais. Three young women sat in place, Mary amongst them.

The only test is for you to successfully walk the fire.

Mimi tried not to panic and run away. Her group walked forward in a line, and she made sure to have the last spot. A light blue curtain stood between them and the challenge. Each woman before her passed through, with no hesitation. She figured they were all under the influence of a spell she escaped. Tatiana stood before her and Mimi tapped her on the arm.

"Aren't you nervous?"

Tatiana turned around and sneered at her.

"It obviously won't be you. It's a harmless prank, you imbecilic."

She turned back around. Mimi fought the temptation to shove her. As the snarky woman walked through the curtain, Mimi snuck closer and peeked. Tatiana walked over the fire and only when she reached the end did anything happen. A spout of flame shot up, and when it receded it left a pile of ash.

Mimi took a step back and desperately looked around. She paused longer and tried to find her escape.

"Come along, dear. It's not as if you have any choice," Ella called to her.

Mimi sighed and hoped it wouldn't hurt too badly. She took a tentative step, and found the glowing coals cool. Even more impossible, she didn't wobble on her heels once. She knew what waited her at the end, and walked slowly with her head high. If death waited for her, she would meet it face to face.

She walked down waiting for the last embrace of fire against her skin. Nothing happened as she passed the end and stepped off the box of coals.

"It would seem you have passed the second test."

"What was the first test?" she asked Ella.

"Being accepted. Join us at the table."

Mimi walked up and took the empty seat next to Mary, who didn't acknowledge her. A clearing of a throat made her look towards the head of the table.

"Salute," Ella said and took a sip after raising her glass.

The four women sitting at the table followed suite. Two fell over immediately, leaving only Mary and Mimi.

"Well this is unusual," Ella said. "Only one of you should be left."

"What did you do to them?" Mimi asked.

"Used a potion to see if they were the one we wanted. They weren't."

"I think Mary and I will just leave," Mimi said standing. She took Mary's hand and pulled.

"Not so fast," a male voice said.

Mimi looked up at the dark haired stranger, who leaned over and pecked Ella on the forehead. He took a knife that had been sitting on the table. He walked over and before Mimi could think, pricked both she and Mary's fingers.

There was no blood on Mimi's finger, just a small scratch. She looked at Mary who stared at her hand. A bead of blood pooled at the tip of her finger.

"She's the one," the man said. "This one belongs with her friends."

"You have Kari and Kelli?" Mimi demanded more than she asked.

"Of course, don't worry they are fine," the man said.

"Dib, will I see you again?" Ella asked.

"Of course darling, we still have a business arrangement," Dib said. "Now, make sure Mary is delivered. Mimi, you can come with me."

Mimi tried to run. In every incarnation of her tales, she'd been a fighter and smart. She dashed around the table, grabbing for anything to use as a weapon. She found nothing, so ran back toward the forest. She made it around the curtain before her world swayed. She stumbled and fell to the ground.

"Well, I guess if we had waited, the wine would've worked," Ella said standing over her.

Mimi felt herself lifted and looked into Dib's dark eyes.

"Don't worry; it will all be over soon."

Her eyes fluttered closed and darkness drove the panic away.

Roll out the red

Red stared a thousand deaths at her computer screen. With a sigh of disgust and a roll of her shoulders, she stood up. She had been starting at lines of code for hours and still couldn't find the hackers code signature. She stalked out of her room and toward the kitchen, intending to find something to eat. Music greeted her from the living room area and despite having failed for the fourth day in a row with code; she smiled as a fond memory surfaced

Only a few months ago, her life had been simple. She had a great schedule—first class at ten, work and then she would allow her roommates to convince her to go dancing. The world could be falling apart and still they would go out to the club.]

She smiled and allowed the memory to push forward. After all the craziness, she welcomed reliving the good times.

Kelli, Kari and Mimi swiveled and gyrated in time to the dubstep music blaring from the great room. Red joined them and felt stress roll of her shoulders as she willed herself to think about nothing. She knew her friends planned to head out to Glamour and listen to their favorite - DJ Jacobi – and have some subpar beer. She knew they would ask her to join, but wasn't sure if she should. She had an assignment to finish. She walked as quietly as possible. The music ended and she almost made it out of the living room.

"You need to grab food before we leave, Red?" Kari asked her.

Ebony colored eyes drilled into her own brown, and Redmondi knew she would give in.

"You are the worst roomie, ever," she said. "If I don't finish this assignment, you have to pay my bills."

"Done. You know I had a great pay day," Kari said. "Go grab dinner, the girls and I will pick out an outfit for you."

"How about you fix me a plate," Red said. "I'm grown enough to pick up my own outfit."

"So you trust us with your food, just not your clothes?"

"You would rather swallow a big hairball than serve crappy food. You can't even serve something with sloppy plating."

Kari hissed at her and she laughed.

Two hours later, she was nice and full of steak, mushrooms and asparagus. She also wore black leggings, a tunic dress top and cute ballet flats. Her roommates had rolled their eyes and thrown much shade at her choice to wear a short cape. She raised an eyebrow and waited.

"I can stay home if I am going to wreck your party," she said.

"No way," Kelli said. "Last time you did that, these two made me the awkward third wheel. With you along, I won't be alone."

"I might find a guy to dance with…"

The raucous laughter from her friends drowned out her very feeble protest. Red turned on her heel, grabbed keys out of the bowl and walked out of the door. The pristine black Jeep Renegade sat in the drive, waiting for her.

"Don't think so," Kelli said, coming out the door after her. "Only I drive my car."

"What if you get drunk?"

"And what if you decide to go home with a guy?" Kelli threw back. "Get in if you want front, those two are coming."

As they drove down I-75 south, the car was a mix of loud music, loud singing and the occasional curse as the car hit potholes. The twenty minute drive was uneventful and refreshing for Red and she began to look forward to her time on the dance floor. She had been working hard for weeks as she tried to find the black hat hacker who stayed just slippery enough, that she couldn't identify him. She was grateful that her friends had pulled her out of her room.

They pulled up to valet, and the girls got out. The line was long and winding in front of the club. But the VIP entrance was empty. Red was thankful that owner owed Kelli many favors and they never had had to wait in the line. They also had access to the second floor, which held the private dance floor. It was nice to be connected. As they walked the two flights of stairs, Red looked back at Kari. Her friend wore six inch stiletto heeled boots, and winked at her.

"I would break my damn ankle," Red muttered. "Flats will forever be my go to."

"Whatever. You know boots are my calling card," Kari said, as she passed her on the steps. "Someday I will teach you how to wear them."

The women made it to their favorite booth, but before their butts made it to the seats the music changed and Gretchen squealed.

"Floor, now," she commanded.

Red grinned as she followed her friends onto the dance floor. She decided to let go of the stress for the evening and just enjoy herself. For the rest of the night, she relaxed and counted on the problem eventually working itself out.

Red shook her head. Since then, all three of her roommates had been kidnapped. None of the information they found after their own quests had been recovered either. The big bad something was slated to arrive any day. And FGM couldn't help with any of it, because she was off looking for her charge.

Red walked to the kitchen, grabbed a bottle of wine, and got ready to watch a movie. Her brain couldn't make sense of anything, and she needed a break. Somewhere around 4 in the morning, she bolted upright in bed. The answer had surfaced as she slept. She grabbed for the notebook, ever present by her bed and scrawled notes before passing back out.

When she woke, she looked at the notes and they still made sense. She got on her computer and started putting the patches. Soon she'd managed to gain access to a private network and she wanted to dance around. If she was correct, this particular network had tendrils reaching out to over five hundred different businesses and power players. She'd found the connections before she found the network. Red was amazed how they all worked, whoever had control, was poised to reach out and grab serious power in the Midwestern trade industry.

She just needed to find the private server farm. While keeping information in cloud systems was easier, physical servers were more secure. She wouldn't be able to figure out who the person was until she had access to all the files. But, she had been able to trace a few lines enough to get a location lock.

Red grabbed the keys to Kelli's jeep.

"I'm coming girls," she muttered. "And yes, I will fill the tank up Goldi. One of us needs to get a car."

Something felt wrong as soon as she turned off the main street in their trendy little college town and into a back alley, which is where the almighty internet said she'd find Ya's. Red had driven through a trendy neighborhood six times, before she finally found the signal. Why make the business so hard to find? If it was supposed to be a cover for the farm, it would make more sense to promote it. She would've never guessed a server farm would be housed in a former industrial warehouse. The farm would need a lot of space, and tracking the massive use of energy should've been obvious.

The main street tried hard to scream its cultural inclusion with the myriad of trendy restaurants stacked on top of each other and fighting for space and top billing. She had to circle around the block twice before she found a place to park on a side street. When she finally got out, she found the streets packed full of people she hadn't expected to be there.

"Why? Why me? I'm on the side of good, dammit," she grumped as she fed quarters into the parking meter.

Red sighed and walked with her head down. Despite it being a Thursday, there was a New Age crystal fair in full swing. She tried her best to walk in the middle of the groups of tourists and avoid eye contact. She hurried her pace and projected the aura of giving her wide berth and she kept her fists balled up by her side. No, she didn't want a tarot reading—especially with grungy energy clinging to them. Nor did she want lucky crystals with all the energy sucked out of them already. The only thing that made her hesitate was the offer of cotton candy.

She walked into Ya's and looked around. The door shut quietly behind her and she realized it was the most secure place she had ever been inside. The door had been set surprisingly well on its hinges so it closed firmly, and there were no windows. Instead clever flat screens projected calm scenery, probably from Nepal. A young woman sat behind a small desk, singing gently under her breath. She gave Red a dazzling smile and stood. Red didn't know what to say, because she expected a dark cool server farm, not a…a business.

"Welcome to Ya's. Are you here to apply for the barista position?"

Red pasted a smile on her face. She wasn't sure what she had expected to find, but a coffee shop wasn't it; although she could appreciate the quirk. Computer geeks did drink a lot of coffee. She couldn't wait to meet the master who created the network; they had a wicked sense of humor.

"I came for a cup of coffee," Red used the key phrase she'd found hidden in code.

The woman's chin length hair slanted to the side with the movement of her head. Confusion covered her doll like face.

"You look like a server."

The soft phrase made Red want to laugh, because the girl made the phrase sound like a question. Then she wondered if it had been deliberate. If nothing else, tongue in cheek had been the feel of the lines of code. Wide eyes blinking at her, reminded her that it was her turn.

"I'm here looking for Lyall," she said. "He has a job for me."

"Oh, I didn't realize you were here for *that* job. You don't look the type."

Says the one looking like a kewpie doll, who probably is a martial arts master. Oh come on Red, stop with the stereotypes, I'm sure she thinks I look like a hood. I shoulda wore my cape.

"Walk through the lavender curtain and knock on the door.

• • •

82

Red almost lost the battle with the beaded curtain, but made it through without flailing, too much. Red tried not to recoil as she walked through another door that shut tightly. The room smelled stale, of spoiled milk, and what she found suffocating and musky … something, she figured would keep people off kilter. The oddly colored lights were another ploy. A kewpie doll with a mocha complexion and wide brown eyes came in and took Red's order for coffee. It was delivered quickly and warmed her stomach pleasantly. The strong taste balanced out some of the layered smells. She looked around the room and felt trapped.

Red held her mug in both hands and looked up as a young man came through the door. Long, silken black hair in a fishtail style cascaded down his back. Her mind had no problem with the hairstyle on the man; he exuded masculinity with each step. He wore a pure white Guayabera shirt. His jeans hung were low on his hips, she figured it was intentional, probably to conceal a weapon. Black hiking boots completed the outfit. He dropped a black leather bag on the back of the chair he straddled to sit.

"Mr. Lyall," she greeted.

"Not at all. I'm his assistant Dib," said the sexy man. "He asked me to meet with you. Do you need anything?"

Wow, why do the bad guys have to be so sexy? It seems like some kind of cliché to make bad look good. Here's hoping Lyall is ugly.

Red bit her bottom lip hard to get her thoughts back in order. She wasn't ashamed of her thoughts, but they would interrupt what she needed to do. If all the clues were correct, her friends were here, as was Mr. Lyall the master mind.

"I'll just wait for my meeting to begin."

"You've impressed us with your skills. You're smart and good with code."

"Thank you," Red said, not sure what else to say.

They sat in quiet until Red thought she would scream. While Dib was a gorgeous companion, he wasn't chatty. As she continued to look around the tiny room, she took in a deep breath and calmed herself. Of course Lyall would want her panicked because then she would make mistakes. She tried to center herself.

A chime sounded, breaking her out of her thoughts.

"It's time. Mr. Lyall is here."

A door slid open in the back of the room. Dib nodded his head toward it. Red took the hint and went toward a dark corridor. She could appreciate the theatrics, but wasn't impressed. Fury overrode everything. Because of this person her life had been turned upside down. Red was a hacker because she liked being alone and quiet. Kidnappings, anxiety, and running all over the city wasn't her style.

She strode down a hallway and into another larger room. There sat her three roommates, gagged and tied to the chairs. A fourth woman, she recognized as Harvey's girlfriend Mary, lay tied to the table. The room was shadowed as oil lamps were the only source of light. She kept moving in and didn't jump when the door shut. A dark figure walked out of the shadows.

"Welcome Red," the voice made her spine crawl. "You can call me Wolf. Lyall, was just a clever cover."

"I really hope you don't expect me to talk about your eyes or teeth. They're not at all impressive."

Wolf smiled. Red would've never figured him for any kind of master mind. He looked sadly normal. Short, balding and pudgy, he hardly seemed like a threat to anyone. However, sayings about wolves in a sheep's clothing came to mind. She knew better than to underestimate her longtime foe.

"Figured it all out?"

"What story about Red Riding Hood wouldn't have a wolf? Props for using Old Norse instead of a language easy to translate," she said.

Wolf nodded and walked to the table. He stroked the face of the young woman. Mimi's eyes narrowed. Red focused on the man in front of her. She wouldn't allow herself to be distracted.

"Let's put the pieces together, shall we?"

Wolf walked behind each of her friends and cut their gags off. Red nervously watched, but never once did he threaten her friends with the knife.

"Oh, I don't want to get rid of you all just yet. I've worked hard on this plan for years. I'm going to brag. As you've figured, it's impossible to escape. The doors are specially fitted, there are no windows, and no one knows you're here."

"Fairy Godmother does," Red said with a rise of her chin.

"Sure she does, but her connection is about to disappear."

"One question first?" Kelli asked. Her voice husky and deep. "Why awaken the princesses?"

"I needed envoys," Wolf said, "Don't rush my story. I'll tell you how it was planned and then show you how it all works."

He pushed the table, still holding the girl toward the wall. He pulled off a red drape, with a wink directed at Red, and revealed a mirror. He untied the woman and propping Mary against him. Her head lolled to the side.

"What we all know, except dear Mary here, is that fairy tales are real. Even in this sad world where magic has been undermined by technology. Which is a great thing for people like me," Wolf said. "Magic is much harder to manipulate. Technology however, is sent out on energy waves that can travel between the realms with no problem. I just had to find a way to get in. Enter those vapid, insipid girls."

Mimi scowled. "I see. You cultivated them to work for you."

"What I did was give them a purpose. The funny thing is how our lives always resemble those damn tales, even when we don't know who we are," Lyall said. "In my realm, I choked to death, but was brought back. My near death experience awakened me to who I really am. I decided I was done getting the short stick. I wanted a new life and decided to figure out how to use the tales to work for me."

Kari groaned. "So you figured out how to use the poor lonely women to help bring you over. You cultivated them from dating site, made them love you and then made them do your bidding."

"And this is why you were taken first. Being a PI meant you could help find the most essential piece, but you were too smart to leave around snooping. You would have figured out the pieces of the whole."

Red felt slightly insulted, she was the heroine of this particular tale.

Wolf held up the antique hand sized spinning wheel. He spun it around in the direct sight line of Mary's face. Fear widened her eyes and she stood frozen. Her face went slack and her eyes vacant.

"No!" Mimi wailed.

Wolf looked into the mirror and spun the wheel again. The pudgy man dropped and Mary shuddered.

"Much better," the soft voice held an edge of malice.

"Okay, let me fill in the rest of the pieces. The wheel pulls souls, the mirror is the place between realms and Mary is the original Grams from this world. The useless life sac lying there was the original wolf, but he had no power here. However, the story anchored to this realm, is one of the tales where I killed Grams and pretended to be her. Making it possible for me to do so again."

Red and the others were transfixed by horror of their situation. Red concentrated on combing through the hundreds of stories in her head for the answer.

"I used the other women to find my artifacts and the right girl. They were lonely, computer illiterate, and easy to control."

Mary walked over to the mirror, took a knife out of a pocket in the dress she wore.

"See? Dress with pockets," Mimi said.

"Mary, fight back," Red said.

The young woman smiled and drove the pommel of the knife into the mirror. Cracks spider webbed out and piece of it fell to the floor.

"Mary's gone. You can never get her back. She's in an empty realm, and in a few hours will fade away. See, when you don't activate the fairy tale life and push out the original personality, you have an empty shell to occupy."

"You killed her," Red said.

"Sure, twice now, in fact," Wolf said. "At least I didn't eat her like I did in the story. Anyhow, I've accomplished my goals, and now it's time for the conclusion."

Red rushed the small woman before she thought about it too hard. She hoped being bigger would be enough, since she had no training in any sort of defense. She swung and punched at the woman; she just wanted to knock the knife out of her hands.

Wolf might have the knowledge of how to use a knife, but Red counted on being heavy enough to pin the body to the ground. When she ended up on the floor with the woman on top of her, she had to rethink her options. She swung wildly, trying to block the knife that kept coming down toward her. She flailed and kicked and managed to dislodge her attacker.

She scooted back toward a wall and reassessed the situation. Red stood up and reached for an antique oil lamp as Wolf moved. The woman was lithe and agile, but cried out like a wounded animal as she brought her knife down with a slash of anger towards Red's thigh.

"Don't let the tales fool you, little girl," the voice snarled into the air. "Just because the boys got a few of the details wrong, doesn't mean that all of them were. How many times did you die in the stories? I did win in the original tale, you know."

Before the knife could be buried deep in her flesh, Red's strong hands caught hold of her enemy's wrists and forced the knife away. Wolf crouched, small and wiry, but incredibly strong. Covered in blood and scratches from their previous tumble, the creature's eyes gleamed with wicked intent in the darkness, all the more eerie as they peered out from a face thrown into shadow and backlit by flickering sconces on the wall.

Red talked to buy time.

"Why not just continue as yourself? Men have more power in this world."

"So they would have you think. Does this form look dangerous? As a man, and an ordinary one at that, I ended up being just another middle aged nobody. But as a cute little thing like this? I will rule them before they realize what's happened," Wolf said, circling around looking for the next striking point. "I learned from them, joined their old boys club, but never got to the top. I know the insides and how to play the game Now I'm going to rule everything."

"Funny to think the Grimm's had to turn you into a wolf to make you less scary."

"Let's get real. Men had learned the lesson early on. Pit the women against each other and the men can rule the world uncontested. It's easy really, this world's design asked for an intercession. As a woman, I have the advantage of looking harmless."

Red had circled the girl around. She had to figure out how to get her friends free and take down Wolf.

"Face it Red, I've already thought of everything. I win again."

"No, Wolf. What you couldn't have counted on is that I have the knowledge. I know all the stories, not just one but they are all memories in my mind. Sometimes I died, true enough. But in every single tale, you are the one to attack," Red said. "Instead of learning, you became evil and bitter. You attacked the helpless, instead of doing what was right. And you're trying to do it here, in this world. But I won't let you. In this world, we women stick together for the greater good."

Wolf's laugh surprised Red. She looked at the other woman, and wondered just how many steps away from crazy she stood.

"Maybe, but my plan is set. You and your little band of merry wenches aren't going to stop me. I've been through hell. I've been the villain in almost every version of our story and I'm done. It's time for me to live my life."

"By killing off another?"

"She didn't even know."

"I know. And she is my family. There's no way I'll let you have her life."

Her lips parted in a sneer and watched fear rise in the woman's eyes. Wolf snarled in response and crouched deeper into the shadows. Her heart was racing with terror and adrenaline. Red rushed forward, scooping up the red drape from the floor. She tackled Wolf with the drape and tangled her in it. The knife slashed out, and Red grabbed for it.

Instead of hoping to subdue the woman, she cut her friends free. Wolf had untangled from the curtains as she cut Kelli, the last one, free. The four were able to subdue the woman after a short scuffle. One on one fighting with a knife had an edge. Four against one, not so much. Kelli and Mimi tied her to a chair.

"Well now what?" Wolf mocked. "You won't kill me or her for that matter. You've got nothing on me. And oh yeah, you can't escape. You're in my stronghold."

Red looked at Wolf and smiled.

"This is where you're wrong. You might have read the stories, but I've lived them all. My story isn't about sexual maturity. Nor about the sexual manipulation of younger women. It's about how Red used cunning to escape. It's a cautionary tale warning against being complacent and unobservant."

Red walked over to the mirror and pulled a broken piece free of the frame. She grabbed the spinning wheel and handed it to Kari.

"I know you thought breaking the mirror would render it useless. You forget it's magic. And all we need is for you to be able to see your eyes. Kari, spin the wheel. In this realm, I win."

Kelli and Mimi held the woman down as she struggled. Kari spun the wheel and Wolf's eyes began to glaze over. Red pushed the mirror in front of her face. Wolf slumped over.

"Is she dead?" Mimi asked.

Red touched her neck.

"Uh, I have no idea how to find a pulse. I'm a hacker, not a nurse."

Kari scoffed and reached over. She sighed in obvious relief and smiled.

"She's breathing."

The women shook her lightly, but nothing happened.

"He did pull her soul out," Kelli said. "How do we put it back in?"

The air shimmered and swirled. FGM appeared. She pushed her silver mane over her should with a smile.

"How did you find us?" Red asked.

"I found Mary," FGM said. "But she just faded away. What happened?"

"She's dead," Mimi sobbed.

"She's not dead, she has a pulse and she's breathing," Kari said.

"Well she won't wake up."

Red launched into an explanation. She detailed Wolf's master plan and described the events. She gave as much detail as she remembered. Wolf may have been an evil bastard, but he'd been thorough. Every detail had been seen to with care. When she finished an air of hopelessness had permeated the room.

"What do we do?" Mimi asked FGM. "Mary is an innocent. She shouldn't have to suffer because Wolf was evil. Harvey loves her."

FGM looked around the circle of women, making eye contact with each of them.

"There is nothing I can do," FGM said softly.

"You're *her* fairy godmother," Kelli said. "There has to be a spell or trick. You kept telling us the reason you could help us because you could only help her. Now do something."

Silence filled the room.

"Wolf only took away the personality tied to this realm. Can't you awaken the fairy tale personality? He didn't do anything with it, because it wasn't active," Red said

Four sets of eyes swung her way.

"Look, we were the first people to have all of our memories awoken, and we're fine."

"She is from a pre-industrial time," FGM said. "She will be out of time and place."
"We'll be here," Kari said. "We will help acclimate her. Goodness knows we've had our share of crazy with all this stuff. Who better to help her?"

The other nodded, but FGM looked wary.

"If we don't try, she's in a coma until her body fails," Kelli said.

"Not to mention, she's my family," Red said.

"She's a bit, um, lighter than you," Mimi said in shock. "You sure you're related?"

"Mixed race babies, all the rage you know," Red sighed in exasperation. "You heard Wolf, she's Grandma from my story. It makes her family. Welcome, by the way, since Harvey is going to be my brother-in-law."

A fall of glitter from the ceiling caught their attention. FGM smiled and picked up a small vial that had materialized.

"Apparently the Council agrees."

The women propped Mary up and FGM fed her the liquid. Mary's eyes blinked a few times.

"Oi, cor! What demons have done this?"

FGM leaned down and whispered in the young woman's ear. Her eyes got wider.

"We're going to need some time," FGM said. "But she'll get there."

Red smiled in relief.

"How about we get out of here?"

Five sets of eyes fixed on FGM.

"You're lucky Mary is here. Hold hands girls."

The women linked hands and smiled. A puff of smoke and a shower of glitter later, they stood in the great room of the house.

"Why glitter?" Kari moaned. "That stuff is impossible to get out of —everything."

"You people came up with the description of fairies, not us."

"I guess we get our Happily Ever After," Red said.

The small chuckle that had started in Red's chest moved up and by the time it came out it was full blown laughter. The other women, aside from Mary who looked at them like they were crazy, joined in until they were out of breath.

"I guess we do," FGM said.

And now the story is yours

Four months later found Kari pacing nervously in front of the house. Her gown swished around her ankles.

"Can you hurry up?" she yelled the question at the house.

"It's not my fault the cat puked on the floor and Red stepped in it," Mimi said, coming down the porch stairs.

"Can someone explain why we didn't make Snow keep the damn thing?" Kelli grumbled. "I've used the lint roller three times already and my gown is covered in white fur."

Red and Mary came out last, with the later trying her best not to break into full laughter. Instead she hid her giggles behind her hand, while Red rolled her eyes.

"Graduation doesn't start for two more hours, you know," she muttered.

"Explain again why there is a celebration for learning how to work?" Mary asked. "It makes no sense, unless your lot just likes to party?"

Red hugged Mary and grinned at her.

"Maybe you'll want to go to school someday. You shouldn't mock our ways."

"Aye, maybe so. Now why are we leaving so early?"

"We need to find parking, there are pictures to be taken, and other stuff." Kari said.

Her roommates just smiled and piled into Kelli's jeep. Mary had settled in nicely, once the women convinced her it would be okay. Mary had caught on quickly and adjusted to all the technology like a pro. She and Red had grown close during the last few months, to no one's surprise.

"Maybe I'm crazy, but I'm glad my senior year was spent with you all," Kelli said.

"You all are like the sisters I never had," Mimi nodded. "Though you are just as needy as Harvey."

The bad news ended up being that one of the side effects of Wolf's plan was that Harvey had to start over with Mary. The new personality didn't know him. The good news was they had only gone on a few dates anyhow. The better news was Mary thought him dashing.

The women chatted as they drove the few blocks to the auditorium for their graduation. As they walked into the building they missed the shimmer of glitter as FGM appeared in front of the parked jeep.

She smiled at the backs of the quintet and softly said "As you have listened and learned, you have grown. And now the story is yours to make as you will."

About the Author

Jennifer Fisch- Ferguson has been writing and publishing fantasy stories since 2003. Publishing credits include writing contests and self-published novels.

She attended the Eastern Michigan University and graduated with a B.A in African American History and promptly went to work with AmeriCorps on a literary initiative. She went to the University of Michigan and got her Master's degree in Public Administration in 2008 and while she finished writing her thesis, also got a Masters in English – Composition and Rhetoric in 2009. She recently is working on her PhD at Michigan State University in the field of Writing and Rhetoric. She has been teaching collegiate and community writing classes since 2003 and loves the variety and inspiration her students bring.

She has an urban fantasy trilogy, a paranormal romance series, and plenty of other new works in progress, along with short stories to fill out her established world. She dutiful writes on her blog space about her journey. She is excitedly expanding her ever developing world and looks forward to the new adventures waiting to be written.

See more at: http://warriorsofluna.com

https://www.facebook.com/ETM.JFF